# ABC
# BOOK

# ABC
# BOOK
# DESIGNED AND
# CUT ON WOOD
# BY C·B·FALLS

BOOKS OF WONDER
MORROW JUNIOR BOOKS
NEW YORK

Published by William Morrow and Company, Inc.
1350 Avenue of the Americas, New York, NY 10019
www.williammorrow.com
Books of Wonder
16 West Eighteenth Street, New York, NY 10011

Printed in Hong Kong by South China Printing Company (1988) Ltd.

10 9 8 7 6 5 4 3 2 1

Library of Congress Cataloging-in-Publication Data
Falls, C. B. (Charles Buckles), 1874–1960.
ABC book / designed and cut on wood by C. B. Falls.
p. cm.—(Books of wonder)
Summary: Presents an animal for each letter of the alphabet,
from antelope and bear to yak and zebra.
ISBN 0-688-14712-7 (trade)—ISBN 0-688-16263-0 (library)
1. English language—Alphabet—Juvenile literature.   [1. Alphabet.]
I. Title.   II. Series.   PE1155.F35 1998   428.1—dc21
[E]   97-47301   CIP AC

A IS FOR ANTELOPE

B IS FOR
BEAR

C IS FOR CAT

D IS FOR DUCK

E IS FOR ELEPHANT

F IS FOR FOX

G IS FOR GIRAFFE

# H IS FOR HORSE

**I** IS FOR IBIS

# J IS FOR JAGUAR

# K IS FOR KANGAROO

L IS FOR LION

M IS FOR MOUSE

# N IS FOR NEWT

O IS FOR ORANG

P IS FOR PELICAN

Q IS FOR QUAIL

R IS FOR ROOSTER

S IS FOR SWAN

T IS FOR TURKEY

U IS FOR
UNICORN

V IS FOR VULTURE

W IS FOR WOLF

# X IS FOR XIPHIUS

Y IS FOR YAK

Z IS FOR ZEBRA

ABCDE
FGHIJK
LMNOP
QRSTU
VWXYZ